# White Fang

## Jack London

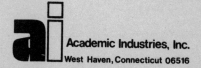

Academic Industries, Inc.
West Haven, Connecticut 06516

*ISBN 0-88301-734-2*

*Published by*
Academic Industries, Inc.
The Academic Building
Saw Mill Road
West Haven, Connecticut 06516

Printed in the United States of America

## about the author

Jack London, who was to become one of the most highly paid authors of his day, was born in 1876, in San Francisco. He was the tenth child in his family, and consequently grew up in poverty. He had to work long hours for little pay; and he fell into the hands of thieves and cutthroats at an early age. In a few years, he turned to drinking as solace for his troubles.

Fortunately, before he was ruined by alcohol, London set sail on a seal ship. By the time he returned to San Francisco, many of his former companions had died. After a brief stint with the railway, London succumbed to his great desire to travel. He spent considerable time in the Klondike region of Alaska, which provided him with a setting for *The Call of the Wild.* Here, too, London encountered the dog after which he modelled his hero, Buck.

The icy regions of Canada's Northwest Territories provided the background for *White Fang.* Here London reverses the previous story and tells a tale of a wolf cub who learns to live in the world of man. It is interesting to note that his animal heroes are always nobler creatures than many of the humans they meet.

In all, Jack London wrote fifty books. Before he died in 1916, they had earned him well over a million dollars.

Jack London

# White Fang

Kiche
Gray Beaver
Beauty Smith
Weedon Scott
White Fang
Bill
Henry

A dark forest grew on both sides of the frozen river. It was cold—the frozen-hearted Northland Wild. It was 50° below zero.
Down the icy river came two living men and a string of dogs pulling a sled. On the sled was a long, narrow box, a coffin holding a dead man.

As the light of the short, sunless day faded, a cry arose on the still air.
A-ow-ooooooooo!
A-ow-OOOOoooo!

They're after us, Bill.
Meat is scarce. I ain't seen a rabbit for days.

*They swung the dogs into a grove of trees and made camp.*

The coffin was used for both seat and table.
Seems to me, Henry, the dogs are staying pretty close to camp.
They know where their hides are safe. They'd sooner *eat* supper than *be* supper.
How many dogs we got, Henry?
Six.
When I was feeding them I took six fish out of the bag. I gave one to each dog. And I was one fish short.
You counted wrong.
I took out six fish! One-Ear didn't get his. I came back for another one for him.
There's only six dogs now.

I saw seven. One of them ran off across the snow.
Then you're thinkin' it was one of them?

Yes. But why didn't the rest of the dogs start to fight it?

A-Ow-OOOOooo!
He was stopped by a long, wailing cry from the darkness.

*In fear, the dogs rushed to the near side of the fire. A circle of gleaming eyes had drawn about the camp.*

How many bullets did you say you had left?
Three, and I wish 'twas three hundred. Then I'd show 'em!

*They slept, rising once in a while to put more wood on the fire. They rose at six o'clock and got ready to leave, though daylight was still three hours away.*

Henry, now there's only five dogs! Fatty's gone!
That's bad!

Once out there, he wouldn't have had a chance. He always was a fool dog.
But no dog would be fool enough to go off that way.

*The men harnessed the remaining five dogs, loaded the sled, and set off. Daylight came at nine o'clock. At three o'clock in the afternoon, the gray light faded and they got ready to make camp again.*

It got half a fish, but I got a whack at it! Did you hear it squeal?
What was it like?

It had four legs and a mouth and looked like any dog. Must be a tame wolf.
He's tame, comin' in here at feeding time for its share of fish!

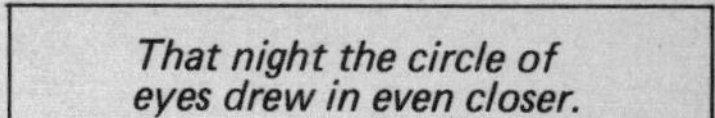
That night the circle of eyes drew in even closer.
I wish they'd find a bunch of moose, then go away and leave us alone.
I wish we were pullin' into Fort McGurry right now!

*The next morning, Henry was awakened by loud cries from Bill.*

What's up now?
Frog's gone!

Frog was the strongest dog of the team!
And no fool dog, either!

That night in camp, Bill worked to keep the dogs safe.
There! That'll fix 'em.
They'll all be here in the morning, all right!

*Later, a sound came from where the dogs were tied.*

Look at that! That fool One-Ear doesn't seem scared!
It's a she-wolf! That explains Fatty and Frog!

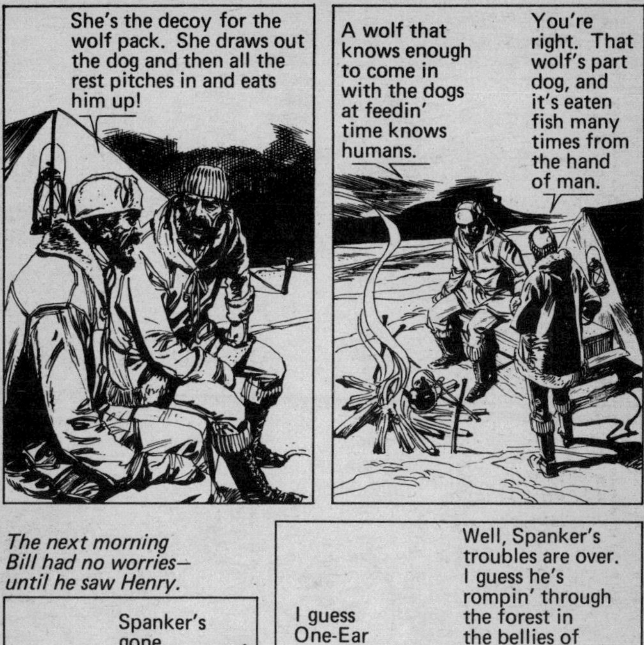
She's the decoy for the wolf pack. She draws out the dog and then all the rest pitches in and eats him up!
A wolf that knows enough to come in with the dogs at feedin' time knows humans.
You're right. That wolf's part dog, and it's eaten fish many times from the hand of man.
*The next morning Bill had no worries— until he saw Henry.*
Spanker's gone.
No! How'd it happen?
I guess One-Ear gnawed him loose.
Well, Spanker's troubles are over. I guess he's rompin' through the forest in the bellies of twenty different wolves.

*About noon that day, Bill took out his rifle.*

You keep right on, Henry. I'm goin' to look around.
You'd better stick by the sled! You've only got three bullets.

*An hour later, Bill caught up again.*

They're keeping up with us and looking for game at the same time. They're sure of us, only they know they've got to wait to get us.
You mean they *think* they're sure of us!

I've seen some of them. They're so thin their ribs are like washboards! They're pretty hungry, I can tell you!

*A few minutes later, Henry gave a low whistle. Bill stopped the dogs.*
Looks just like a big husky sled-dog!
It's the she-wolf!

Henry, it's a dead shot! It's got away with three of our dogs and we ought to put a stop to it. What do you say?
Okay, Bill.
But before Bill could raise the gun to his shoulder, the wolf had leaped away.
Look at that!
I might have known it! A wolf that knows enough to come in with the dogs at feeding time would know all about guns.
But that creature's the cause of all our troubles, and I'm going to get her yet!
Don't stray too far off! If that pack ever jumps you, your three bullets would be worth no more than a drop of water in a cooking fire!

They camped early that night.
I'm tying 'em out of gnawing-range of each other tonight.
Stands to reason three dogs can't pull as far or as fast as six dogs.

*But so near did the wolves come that the dogs were frantic with fear. Bill had to build up the fire often.*

I've heard talk of sharks followin' a ship. Those wolves are *land* sharks!

*The next day began well. They'd lost no dogs overnight. Then at noon the sled overturned.*

Here, One-Ear!

But One-Ear broke into a run. And there out on the snow was the she-wolf waiting for him.
Here, One-Ear! Come back! Stop!

*As he came nearer, the she-wolf seemed to laugh playfully at him.*

Each time he tried to rub noses with her, she pulled away, luring him into danger.

*Too late, One-Ear learned his mistake. A dozen wolves came bounding across the snow to cut off his return to camp.*

Bill! Where are you goin'?
I won't stand it! They ain't going to get any more of our dogs if I can help it!

Gun in hand, Bill plunged into the underbrush beside the trail.
Be careful! Don't take any chances!

*Henry sat down and waited. There was nothing else to do. Somewhere out there Bill, One-Ear, and the wolf pack were coming together.*

*All too quickly it happened. He heard three shots.*

Bang!
Bang!
Bang!

Oh, no! His bullets are gone! Bill don't stand a chance now! That's the last I'll ever see of him.

*There was a great noise of snarls and yelps; One-Ear's yell of pain; the cry of a wolf. And that was all. The yelping died away. Silence settled over the land.*

*At last Henry rose, moving slowly. He harnessed the two remaining dogs, took the axe, and passed a rope over his own shoulder.*

*He made camp early, gathering a good supply of firewood and making his bed close to the fire. But he was not to enjoy that bed.*

*The wolves drew close about him in a narrow circle. It was only a blazing fire that kept them from his body.*

*Bit by bit, inch by inch, the circle would draw closer. Then he would pull burning sticks from the fire and throw them into the pack.*

Take that, you devils!

*At dawn, when the wolf pack drew away, Henry started the job he had planned during the long night.*

I don't understand why a man who's a lord in his own country would come all the way to this icy end of the earth!

He might have lived to a ripe old age in his own country!

Using the sled ropes and with the aid of the dogs, he pulled the coffin to the platform he had built.
They got Bill, and they may get me, but they won't get you, Lord Alfred!

*He took the trail again, the sled bounding over the snow. The starving wolves were bolder, trotting along behind and on either side. He stopped with several hours of daylight still left, and used the time to chop a great supply of firewood.*

*The night was full of danger. Henry stayed by the fire. He tried not to sleep. But the wolves kept coming closer.*

They're like kids waiting around a table to begin— and I'm the food!

*All night he fought them off with burning sticks. For the first time the wolves did not go away at dawn.*

Got to have firewood! I'll get over to that dead tree and chop it down.

*The next night, almost dead on his feet, Henry lost both dogs. As a last move, he built a circle of fire and sat inside. But dawn came, the fire burned low, and there was no more wood.*

Guess you can come and get me any time. Anyway, I'm goin' to sleep!

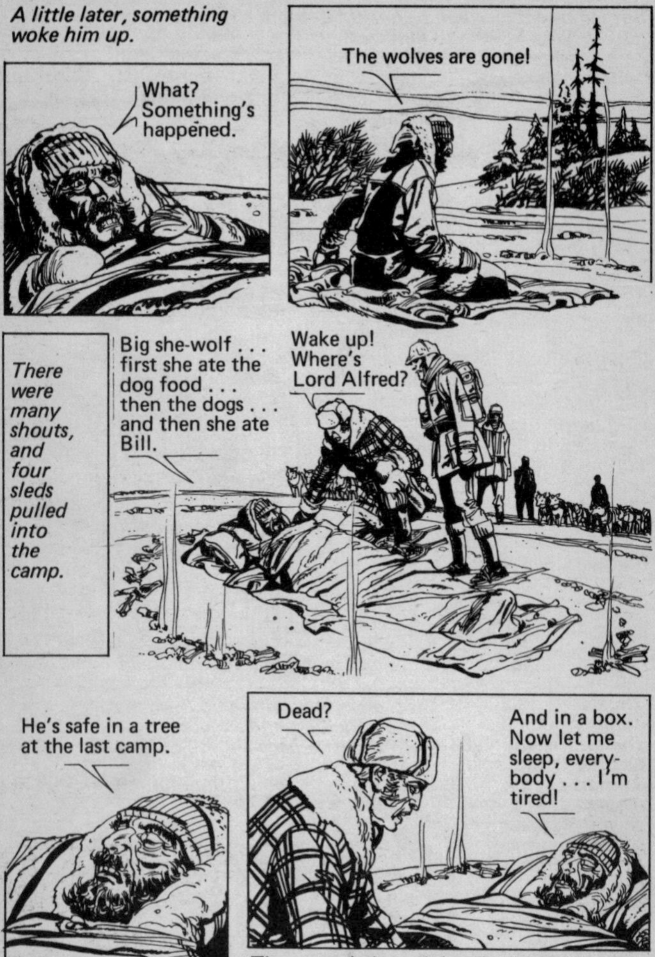
A little later, something woke him up.
What? Something's happened.
The wolves are gone!
There were many shouts, and four sleds pulled into the camp.
Wake up! Where's Lord Alfred?
Big she-wolf . . . first she ate the dog food . . . then the dogs . . . and then she ate Bill.
He's safe in a tree at the last camp.
Dead?
And in a box. Now let me sleep, every-body . . . I'm tired!
The men, sleds, and dogs had driven off the hungry wolves. They were now looking for other food.

*But far away could still be heard the cry of the hungry wolf pack as they followed a new trail.*

A-owww-ooOOOOOOO!

*They ran many miles that day before their search was rewarded. Then they came upon a moose. It was a short fight.*

*The moose weighed 800 pounds. There was food for all. And they had reached a land where there was plenty of game. No longer driven together by hunger, the pack split up. Two by two, male and female, the wolves trotted off.*

*The she-wolf ran with an old, one-eyed wolf on one side, and a big, younger leader on the other.*

*There came a day when the two wolves fought it out while the she-wolf watched.*

*The wisdom of the older wolf won out. When the young wolf lay dead in the snow, One-Eye walked up to the she-wolf.*

*After that they ran side by side, hunting their meat together, killing and eating it. After a time the she-wolf became restless. She seemed to be searching for something.*

*The hollows under fallen trees attracted her.*

*She nosed about the larger cracks in the rocks.*

*She explored caves in the banks of streams.*

*At last she found what she was looking for near a frozen stream that in summer flowed into the Mackenzie River.*

*To get into the cave she had to crawl a few feet.*

*Then the walls widened and rose to form a little round room. It was dry and cozy. After circling a few times, the she-wolf lay down with a tired sigh.*

*One-Eye was hungry. Outside there was an April sun and a feeling of spring. When he failed to interest his mate in moving, he set off alone.*

*Returning eight hours later, he stopped at the cave's mouth. Strange sounds came from within. He moved inside and was met by a warning snarl.*

G-r-r-rrrr!

*One-Eye had fathered cubs many times before in his long life. But each time it was a fresh surprise. After a few hours' sleep, he left again to hunt food for his family.*

*Their eyes still closed, the cubs came to their mother for milk and a warm, soothing tongue.*

*After they could move, they found she had paws that could roll them over if they crawled too near the mouth of the cave.*

*Four of the cubs were a reddish color like their mother. One little cub was pure gray, a real wolf like old One-Eye.*

He was the strongest of the litter, the first to learn to roll another over with a paw-stroke.

*It was he who first grabbed another by the ear and pulled and tugged.*

Grr-rrr-r-r!

Then hunger struck the land. The cubs slept most of the time. There was no meat at all in the countryside. She-wolf left her litter to hunt food for them. One-Eye ranged far and wide.
At last One-Eye died in a fight with a lynx.

*When there was food again, only gray cub and his mother were left.*

*The cubs had been taught to stay away from the mouth of the cave. But gray cub was growing and exploring. One day when he was alone he went to the edge of the hole and saw the world!*

*Suddenly he tumbled head over heels down the slope.*

Ki-yi-yi-yi!

At the bottom he stopped and looked around. He was very frightened.
But nothing happened. So he stood up and licked the dust off his fur.
He set out to explore. A squirrel startled him.
Grr-r-r-r-r . . .
But the squirrel, just as scared, ran up a tree.
With beginner's luck, he stumbled into a ptarmigan's nest full of chicks.
Cheep! Cheep! Cheep! Cheep!

*He picked one up in his mouth. It tasted good. He ate it. He ate all the chicks, then licked his chops. He was a hunter! At last he began to feel sleepy. He set out to look for the cave.*

In his path he saw a small, live thing—a baby weasel.

Then he heard a high frightening squeal. The mother weasel attacked.

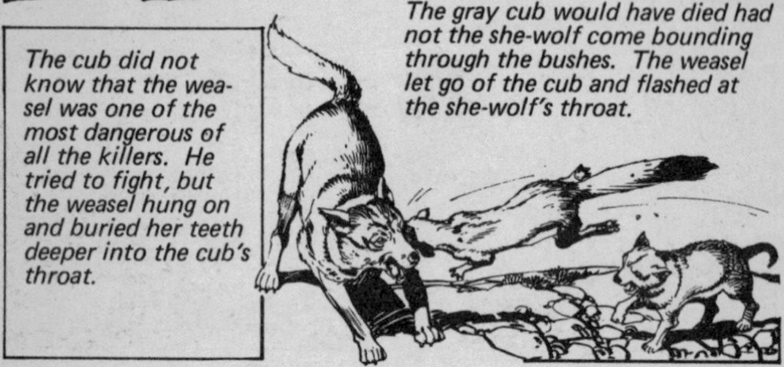
The cub did not know that the weasel was one of the most dangerous of all the killers. He tried to fight, but the weasel hung on and buried her teeth deeper into the cub's throat.
The gray cub would have died had not the she-wolf come bounding through the bushes. The weasel let go of the cub and flashed at the she-wolf's throat.

*Snapping her head like a whip, the she-wolf tossed the weasel into the air, then caught it between her jaws and killed it.*

The she-wolf and her cub touched noses. Then between them they ate the weasel and went back to the cave and slept.

*One day he came across some creatures he had never seen before.*

*So the gray cub grew and learned the law:* eat or be eaten. *But the greatest change, his biggest lessons, were still to come.*

*Something told him that man, the two-legged animal, was lord over all living things. He was afraid.*

Look! White fangs!
Go on! Pick him up!

*A hand touched the cub. His teeth snapped. He sent them into the hand.*

*Angrily the man hit him, knocking him over.*

All the fight left him. He sat up and cried.
A-ow-oooooooo!
In his fright he heard something. The Indians heard it, too. His mother was coming, snarling as she ran.
Gr-r-r-r-r-r!
The she-wolf bounded in among them. The cub leaped to meet her. The Indians backed up.
Gr-r-r-r-r-r!
One of the men called out in surprise. The cub felt his mother start at the sound.
Kiche! Kiche!

*The cub saw his mother crouching, wagging her tail, making peace signs. She did not snap when the men put their hands on her.*

She ran away a year ago in the time of hunger when there was no meat for the dogs.
She has lived with the wolves!

And this cub is the sign of it! It is not so strange. Kiche's mother was a dog, but her father was a wolf!

In him there is little dog and much wolf! His fangs are white, and White Fang shall be his name!

*Gray Beaver tied Kiche to a tree, and White Fang lay down beside her. Soon the rest of the tribe trailed into camp. With them were many dogs. With a rush, they attacked White Fang.*

In a few seconds he was on his feet again. He watched the man-animals drive back the dogs.
He began to know man as the one who makes and carries out the law.

The Indians continued their march. A tiny man-animal led Kiche, and White Fang followed. After a long journey they made camp at the Mackenzie River.

White Fang was interested in everything. He watched Gray Beaver do something with sticks and dry moss.

All right, White Fang! Come close!

Suddenly a strange thing like mist rose from beneath Gray Beaver's hands.
A live thing appeared, twisting and turning, the color of the sun. White Fang touched it with his nose—and drew back in fear and pain.
YIIIiiiiiii!
So he learned about fire, and that man was the fire-maker.
A part-grown puppy larger and older than White Fang known as Lip-lip became White Fang's enemy. Whenever he moved away from his mother Kiche, the bully would appear and start a fight.
White Fang could not beat Lip-lip. But he was forced to become a good fighter.
One day Gray Beaver traded Kiche to Three Eagles.
A strip of cloth, a bearskin, twenty bullets—and Kiche!
Good! All will be useful on my trip to Great Slave Lake!

White Fang saw his mother taken aboard Three Eagles' canoe. The canoe shoved off. He jumped into the water and followed.
Here! White Fang! Come back!

Gray Beaver angrily started after him. Catching up to White Fang, he pulled him from the water and hit him.

When White Fang crawled ashore, weak and tired, Lip-lip rushed upon him. Too helpless to defend himself, it would have gone hard with White Fang. But Gray Beaver's foot shot out, tossing Lip-lip through the air.

This was man's law again. White Fang was grateful. He learned that man kept for himself the right to punish.

Soon White Fang learned to get along with Gray Beaver—man. He learned to obey. And when he obeyed he was not hurt.
Indeed, Gray Beaver himself sometimes tossed Fang some meat. He even defended him against the other dogs in eating it.
But he was still lonely for Kiche and longed for her return. He missed the free life of the Wild.

*In the fall, his chance came. The Indians broke their summer camp. They took down tepees, loaded canoes, prepared for the fall hunting.*

He waited for a chance to creep out to the woods. Then he ran through a stream to hide his trail.

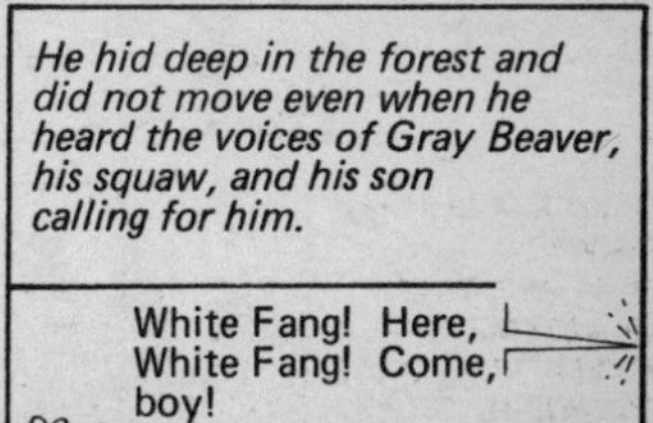
He hid deep in the forest and did not move even when he heard the voices of Gray Beaver, his squaw, and his son calling for him.
White Fang! Here, White Fang! Come, boy!

*The voices died away. Night came. After a while he crept out of his hiding place. It was cold—and lonely.*

*A tree cracked above him. He grew frightened. Madly he ran toward the village.*

YIIIiiii!

*He wanted campfires and food, but the village had gone. Where Gray Beaver's tepee had stood, he sat and pointed his nose at the moon.*

A-ow-ow-ow-OOOO-OOOOO!

*At dawn he made up his mind. He took the trail downriver.*

*For thirty hours White Fang ran without food or rest. Sometimes he climbed mountains and swam the mouths of rivers that entered the main river.*

He was weak and limping, the pads of his feet sore and bleeding.

It began to snow as he stumbled along. Then suddenly he struck the fresh scent he searched for.

*It was Gray Beaver's camp! The Indians had killed a moose on White Fang's side of the river. White Fang smelled the campfire, heard voices. He crawled straight to Gray Beaver, expecting to be punished.*

It's White Fang!

Instead of hitting him, Gray Beaver gave him meat and guarded him from the other dogs as he ate.

*Later, White Fang lay by the fire at Gray Beaver's feet, content.*

Of his own choice he had come to sit by man's fire and be ruled by him.

*Soon White Fang learned to be a sled dog. First with other puppies, he was harnessed to the sled of Mit-sah, Gray Beaver's son. Lip-lip, the largest of the young dogs, was the team leader.*

Hi! Hup! Gee!
White Fang took well to the work. He pulled hard and obeyed orders.

*The years passed. White Fang grew and filled out. He learned more about fighting. He became not only the head of the team, but the ruler of the other dogs. He made no friends among his own kind, but led them by his bravery and skill.*

*He went on long journeys with Gray Beaver. In every village, when other dogs growled at him, he fought them and won.*
Never was there such an animal! He is strongest and quickest of all dogs!
He has proved this by his killings among our best dogs.

*In his fourth summer, White Fang went with Gray Beaver to Fort Yukon. It was 1898. Thousands of gold hunters were passing through on their way to the Klondike.*

I have brought many furs; also mittens and moccasins to sell.
You are wise! Much money can be made here!

For the first time, he saw white men.
Look at that, would you? Looks like a wolf!
Be careful he doesn't take off your hand!

*Few white men lived in the Yukon. But steamships brought more of them—and their dogs—to the gold fields.*

*White Fang soon saw that the white men were more powerful than the Indians but that their dogs were not. As soon as they saw White Fang they would rush at him. He would fight the attacker, then leave him for the Indian dog pack to finish off. But the white men would always rush to the rescue of their own dogs.*

Among the few white men who lived at the fort was "Beauty" Smith. He was given that name because he was so ugly.
Watch out, Beauty! That wolf'll eat you up!
He's great, isn't he? A real killer! I want that dog!
White Fang was there when Beauty first visited Gray Beaver's camp. Right away he sensed the evil in the man.
How much will you take for that dog?
White Fang? He's the strongest sled dog I've ever owned! There isn't a dog like him in the whole Yukon!
He can fight! He kill other dogs like man kills a fly. He's not for sale at any price!
I like him! I want him!
Smith came back again and again—bringing a bottle or two of whiskey under his coat.
This fire-water gives me thirst! The more I drink, the more I want.
Drink up, man! Plenty more where that came from!

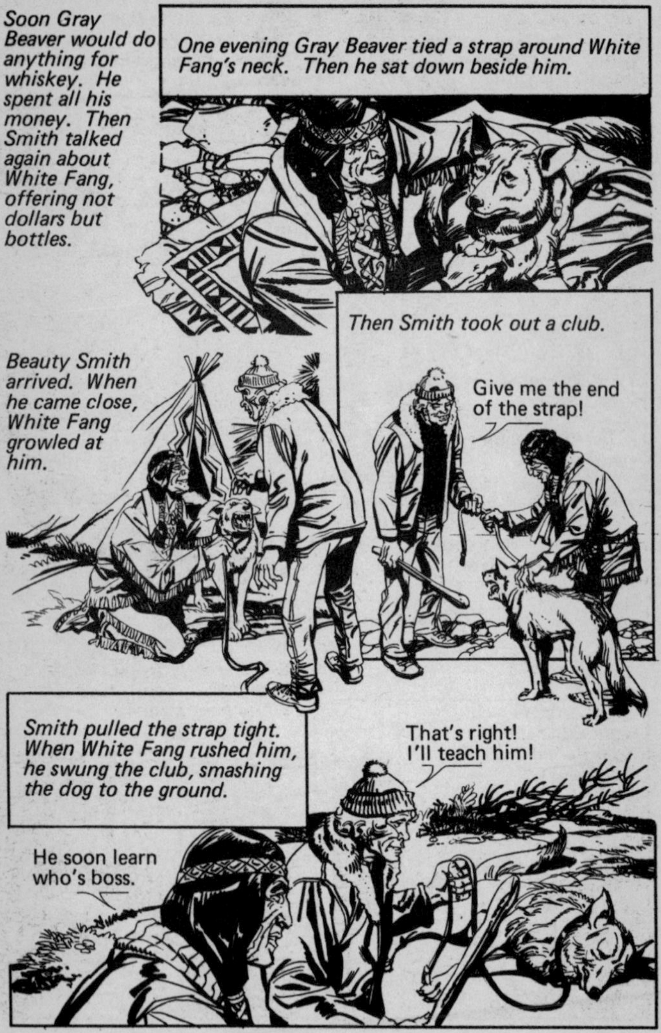
Soon Gray Beaver would do anything for whiskey. He spent all his money. Then Smith talked again about White Fang, offering not dollars but bottles.
One evening Gray Beaver tied a strap around White Fang's neck. Then he sat down beside him.
Beauty Smith arrived. When he came close, White Fang growled at him.
Then Smith took out a club.
Give me the end of the strap!
Smith pulled the strap tight. When White Fang rushed him, he swung the club, smashing the dog to the ground.
That's right! I'll teach him!
He soon learn who's boss.

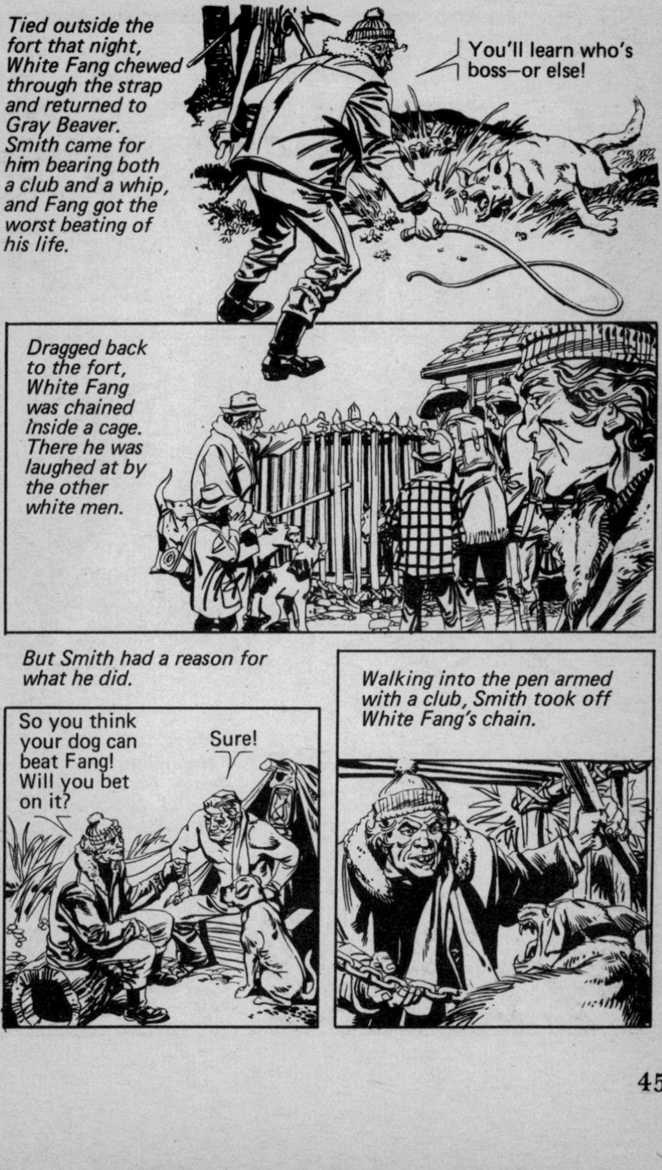
Tied outside the fort that night, White Fang chewed through the strap and returned to Gray Beaver. Smith came for him bearing both a club and a whip, and Fang got the worst beating of his life.
You'll learn who's boss—or else!
Dragged back to the fort, White Fang was chained inside a cage. There he was laughed at by the other white men.
But Smith had a reason for what he did.
So you think your dog can beat Fang! Will you bet on it?
Sure!
Walking into the pen armed with a club, Smith took off White Fang's chain.

*The pen door was opened again. A large dog was pushed inside.*

Go get him, boy!

Here was something on which White Fang could spend his hate! He sprang.

The men outside cheered the fight. There was no hope for the other dog. In the end, while Smith beat back White Fang, he was dragged out by his owner.

*Then Smith was paid for his bet. Money clinked into his hand.*

I don't think anything can beat that dog of yours!
The Fighting Wolf—that's what you should call him!

*Soon White Fang had beaten every dog around. Smith took him by steamship up the Yukon to Dawson where men paid fifty cents in gold dust to see him. He beat full-grown wolves. Finally he fought for his life against a full-grown lynx—and won.*

After that, for a while, there were no more fights—until Tim Keenan reached town.
Say, mister, what kind of dog is that?
That's Cherokee. Guess he's the first bulldog ever to enter the Klondike.
Don't suppose he can fight?
Fight? That's just what he's for!
A fight was set up, and on the stated day a crowd gathered to watch.
Sic'm, Cherokee! Go to it! Eat 'm up!

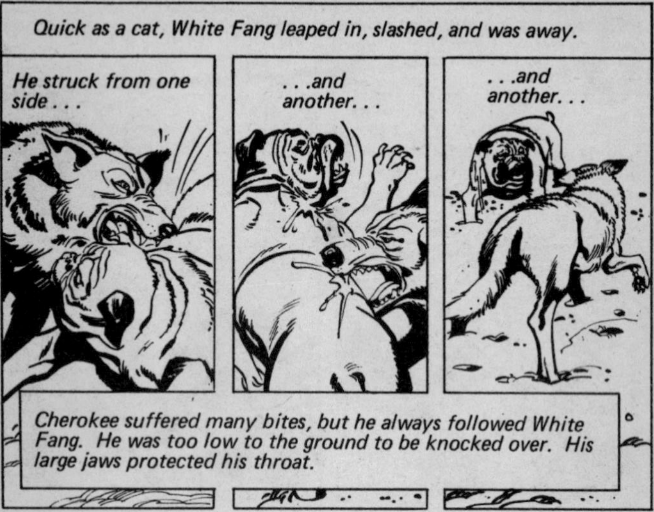
Quick as a cat, White Fang leaped in, slashed, and was away.
He struck from one side . . .
. . .and another. . .
. . .and another. . .
Cherokee suffered many bites, but he always followed White Fang. He was too low to the ground to be knocked over. His large jaws protected his throat.

*At last, in one of White Fang's charges, Cherokee got a grip on White Fang's throat—and held on. Fang whirled round and round. He pulled Cherokee off his feet, but nothing could loosen his grip. Finally White Fang was down.*

Fang! Get up and fight!

White Fang was choking from lack of air. Smith, mad with anger, began to kick him. Suddenly two strangers burst through the crowd.
You brute!
With a blow of his fist, Weedon Scott knocked Smith flat. Then he and his friend Matt knelt beside the dogs.
Can't break 'em apart this way, Mr. Scott. You'll have to pry them loose.
Pulling out his gun, Scott forced it between Cherokee's teeth.
Bit by bit Scott loosened the jaws until White Fang's neck was free.
Just about all in, but he's still breathing!

What's a good sled-dog worth, Matt?
Three hundred dollars. And a chewed-up one like this is worth half of that.
I'm taking your dog, and I'm giving you a hundred and fifty for him.
I ain't selling! The dog's a gold mine! A man's got his rights!

You're not a man! You're a beast! Will you take the money, or shall I hit you again?

*Taken to Scott's cabin, given rest and food, White Fang soon got better. But he still feared and hated men.*

He's a fine animal. But I'm afraid no one can tame him!
Look what men have done to him! It will take time, but kindness will win him over.

*There was kindness in Scott's voice, and kindness in his touch. At last Fang allowed himself to be petted. After a while came a feeling he had never known before: love for his master.*

I never thought I'd see the day! But I don't know what he'll do when you go south. You're his god!
I know, Matt. But I can't take a wolf home. to California!

*His work as a mining expert over, Scott was ready to go home. Somehow White Fang knew it. For the first time the two men heard Fang give his wolf-howl.*

A-owww-OOO-OOOOOOOO!
Listen to that! He's crying! He's stopped eating, too. Beats me how he knows!
But it would be impossible to take him to California!

The morning came when Scott was to leave. The steamboat waited at the dock.
You're sure White Fang's locked inside?
Yessir! Locked up tight!

On deck, Scott and Matt said goodbye.
Goodbye, Matt. Be sure to write me how White Fang gets along!
Look! It's him!
Look, Scott! Fresh cuts on his face, and all over his stomach!
Guess he broke right through the window, glass and all!
Guess I can use this to drag him ashore.
No! White Fang's going to California with me!

*Landing in San Francisco, White Fang found it a nightmare. The streets were full of dangers. There were wagons, carts, automobiles. The cable and electric cars never stopped their clanging.*

It's all right, old boy.
Just stick close to my heels.

*Tied in a corner of a baggage-car, he thought he had been left behind until he sniffed out the master's luggage. Then he stood guard over it.*

That dog of yours won't let me lay a finger on your stuff!
It's all right, Fang. We get off here.

*The nightmare city had been left behind. Outside was quiet countryside and a waiting coach.*

Mother! Dad!
Weedon! At last you're here!

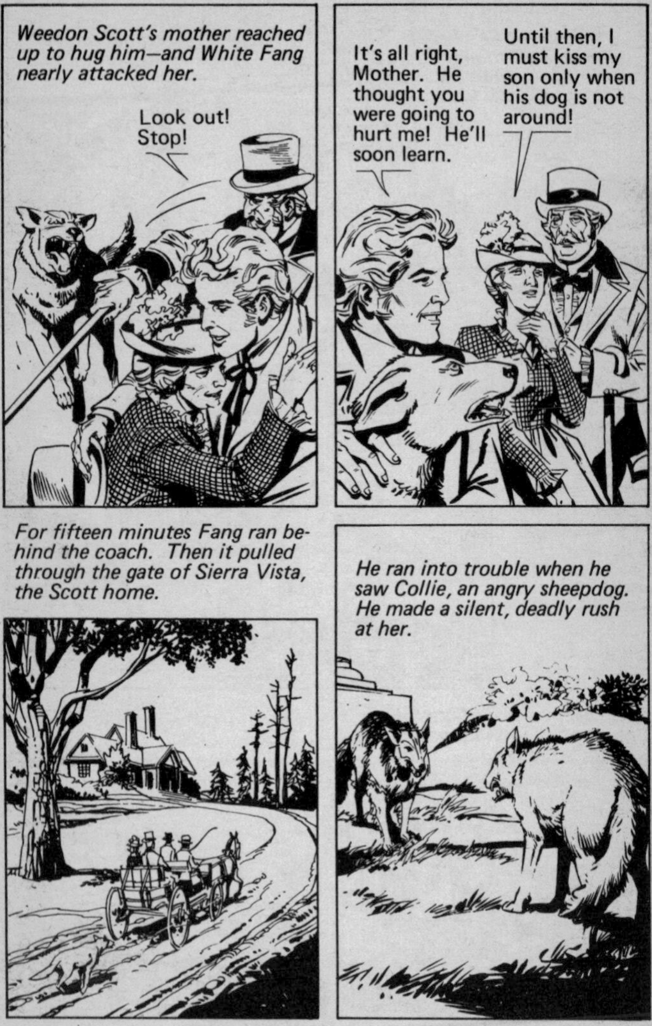
Weedon Scott's mother reached up to hug him—and White Fang nearly attacked her.
Look out! Stop!
It's all right, Mother. He thought you were going to hurt me! He'll soon learn.
Until then, I must kiss my son only when his dog is not around!
For fifteen minutes Fang ran behind the coach. Then it pulled through the gate of Sierra Vista, the Scott home.
He ran into trouble when he saw Collie, an angry sheepdog. He made a silent, deadly rush at her.

But Collie was a female! He stopped short. He knew he must not attack.

*But Collie knew she should hate and fear wolf-like animals. For many months she would nip at White Fang whenever he came near.*

But all he ever did was bowl her over.

*Fang was a very smart dog. And he would do anything to please his master. So as the months passed, he learned many new things. Among the first was to love his master's family.*

*As well as Judge and Mrs. Scott, Weedon's parents, there was the master's wife Alice. They had two children, Weedon and Maud.*

He is so strong! I can't help worrying that he'll hurt the children!
Never, my dear!

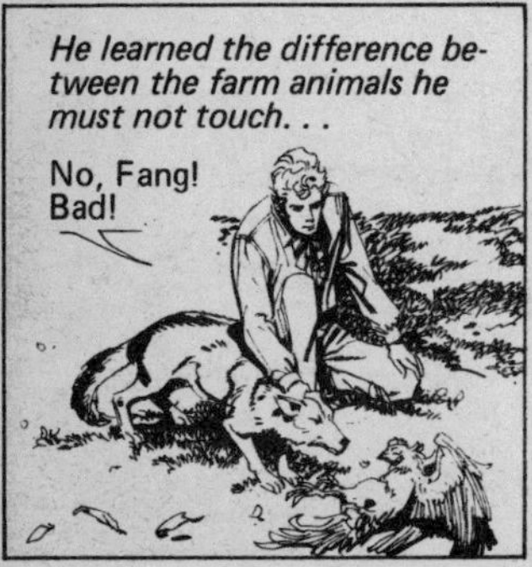
He learned the difference between the farm animals he must not touch. . .
No, Fang! Bad!

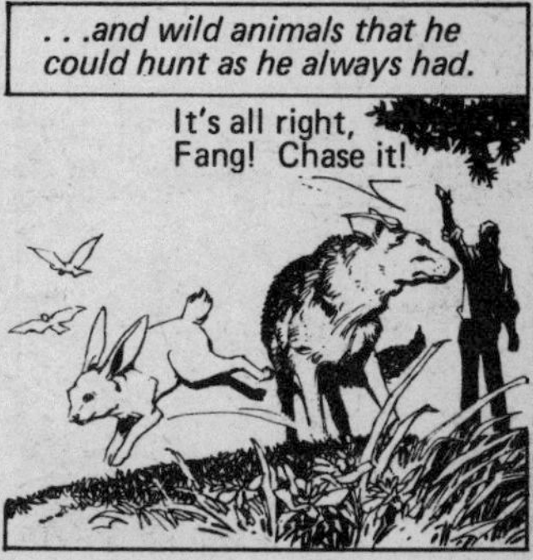
. . .and wild animals that he could hunt as he always had.
It's all right, Fang! Chase it!

To go with Scott when he rode out on horseback was White Fang's greatest joy. One day a horse fell, and Scott's leg was broken.
Go home! Go home and tell them what's happened. Home, Fang!
The family was sitting on the porch when Fang arrived.
Fang! Nice doggie!
But Fang pushed them off, growling, and leaped in front of the judge.
Woof! Woof!
Go away! Lie down, Fang!
Fang turned to Scott's wife. Taking the cloth of her dress in his teeth, he pulled until it tore.
I hope he's not going mad!
No! Something's happened to Weedon! Fang's trying to tell us!
Fang ran down the steps and led them to his master. After this event he found a warmer spot in the hearts of the Sierra Vista family.

Then as the days grew shorter and Fang's second winter in the south came on, he found that Collie's bite no longer hurt. She became playful.

Scott planned to ride one day. His horse stood at the door. White Fang was near.

But when Collie nipped him gently and ran off, he turned and followed. Scott rode alone that day. And White Fang ran with Collie as his mother Kiche had run with One-Eye long years before.

*About that time the newspapers were full of stories about the daring escape of a man named Jim Hall from San Quentin prison.*

Any more news of the escape?
Hall killed three guards. He took their guns with him!
There's a large reward offered for him. But he seems to have disappeared!

I'm really afraid! He stood up in court and swore to kill you when you sentenced him.
Don't worry, my dear! I had no choice but to give him fifty years.
Of course not. But he blames you just the same!

White Fang was not allowed to sleep in the house. But now he and Alice Scott had a secret.
Shhh! Take care of us, Fang!

*Each night she arose and let White Fang in to sleep in the big hall. Each morning, she slipped down and let him out again.*

On one such night, White Fang awoke to sense a strange man moving silently through the hall to the stairs.
Upstairs slept the master and his loved ones. As the man went up, Fang struck.
Turning on the light, Judge Scott and Weedon walked down the stairs.
The family was awakened by terrible noises. There were gunshots, screams, snarls and growls, the smashing of chairs. In three minutes it was over.
Jim Hall! He's dead.
Then they turned to White Fang.
I'm afraid he's done for, poor dog!
We'll see about that! I'll call the best doctor in the state!

After working an hour and a half, the doctor talked to Weedon and Alice.
A broken leg, three broken ribs, three bullet holes right through him—I give him one chance in a thousand.
But White Fang was very strong. The weeks passed. He got well.
The last cast is off now. He'll have to learn to walk again. But take him outside. It won't hurt him.
The Blessed Wolf—that's what we'll call him.
Outside he went, like a king, the whole family around him. He was still very weak, and on the lawn he lay down and rested.
Good boy! Great boy!
The group moved on again. They came to the stables. There in the doorway lay Collie, a half-dozen puppies playing about her in the sun.
Didn't know you were a family man, did you, old boy?

*Collie growled, but the master pushed one puppy toward Fang.*

Look at him, Fang . . . that's your son!

*Their noses touched. White Fang's tongue went out, and he licked the puppy's face. Handclapping and pleased cries came from the family.*

Do you think he knows it's his own puppy?
Of course he does!

*Fang lay down and the other puppies came running to him. As his human gods clapped, they climbed and tumbled over their father. Then Fang closed his eyes contentedly, and took a nap in the sun.*

THE END

## COMPLETE LIST OF POCKET CLASSICS AVAILABLE

### CLASSICS

C 1 Black Beauty
C 2 The Call of the Wild
C 3 Dr. Jekyll and Mr. Hyde
C 4 Dracula
C 5 Frankenstein
C 6 Huckleberry Finn
C 7 Moby Dick
C 8 The Red Badge of Courage
C 9 The Time Machine
C10 Tom Sawyer
C11 Treasure Island
C12 20,000 Leagues Under the Sea
C13 The Great Adventures of Sherlock Holmes
C14 Gulliver's Travels
C15 The Hunchback of Notre Dame
C16 The Invisible Man
C17 Journey to the Center of the Earth
C18 Kidnapped
C19 The Mysterious Island
C20 The Scarlet Letter
C21 The Story of My Life
C22 A Tale of Two Cities
C23 The Three Musketeers
C24 The War of the Worlds
C25 Around the World in Eighty Days
C26 Captains Courageous
C27 A Connecticut Yankee in King Arthur's Court
C28 The Hound of the Baskervilles
C29 The House of the Seven Gables
C30 Jane Eyre
C31 The Last of the Mohicans
C32 The Best of O. Henry
C33 The Best of Poe
C34 Two Years Before the Mast
C35 White Fang
C36 Wuthering Heights
C37 Ben Hur
C38 A Christmas Carol
C39 The Food of the Gods
C40 Ivanhoe
C41 The Man in the Iron Mask
C42 The Prince and the Pauper
C43 The Prisoner of Zenda
C44 The Return of the Native
C45 Robinson Crusoe
C46 The Scarlet Pimpernel

## COMPLETE LIST OF POCKET CLASSICS AVAILABLE (cont'd)

C47 The Sea Wolf
C48 The Swiss Family Robinson
C49 Billy Budd
C50 Crime and Punishment
C51 Don Quixote
C52 Great Expectations
C53 Heidi
C54 The Illiad
C55 Lord Jim
C56 The Mutiny on Board H.M.S. Bounty
C57 The Odyssey
C58 Oliver Twist
C59 Pride and Prejudice
C60 The Turn of the Screw

## SHAKESPEARE

S 1 As You Like It
S 2 Hamlet
S 3 Julius Caesar
S 4 King Lear
S 5 Macbeth
S 6 The Merchant of Venice
S 7 A Midsummer Night's Dream
S 8 Othello
S 9 Romeo and Juliet
S10 The Taming of the Shrew
S11 The Tempest
S12 Twelfth Night